Ladybird Readers

Peter Rabbit
and the
Radish Robber

Series Editor: Sorrel Pitts
Text adapted by Sorrel Pitts

LADYBIRD BOOKS

UK | USA | Canada | Ireland | Australia
India | New Zealand | South Africa

Ladybird Books is part of the Penguin Random House group of companies
whose addresses can be found at global.penguinrandomhouse.com.
www.penguin.co.uk   www.puffin.co.uk   www.ladybird.co.uk

First published 2017
001

Printed in China

A CIP catalogue record for this book is available from the British Library

ISBN: 978-0-241-29742-1

All correspondence to
Ladybird Books
Penguin Random House Children's
80 Strand, London WC2R 0RL

Ladybird Readers

Peter Rabbit and the Radish Robber

Based on the
Peter Rabbit™ TV series

Picture words

 Peter Rabbit

 Lily

 Benjamin

Cotton-tail

4

Mr. McGregor

Squirrel
Nutkin

Mr. Tod

radishes

Peter Rabbit and Benjamin
go to Mr. McGregor's garden.
They want some radishes.

Mr. McGregor sees them!

"Run!" says Peter.

The two rabbits run
from Mr. McGregor.

They have got
three radishes.

Peter and Benjamin go back to Peter's house.

"Go and play," says Peter's mother.

Peter and Benjamin
see Lily.

"Would you like a radish,
Lily?" says Peter.

"Yes please,"
says Lily.

13

"Where is my radish?"
says Lily.

"Oh, no!" says Peter.
"We have got two
radishes, now."

"A robber has got mine!"
says Lily.

They go to Squirrel Nutkin's tree.

"Let's eat the radishes here," says Peter.

"No, you cannot eat them here!" says Squirrel Nutkin.

17

Peter goes after
the radishes.

"Oh, no!" says Benjamin.
"Now, we have got one
radish."

19

"Oh, no! It is Mr. Tod!"
says Peter.

"Run!" says Lily.

The three rabbits
run from Mr. Tod.

"We have no radishes
now," says Benjamin.

"A robber has got our radishes," says Lily.

The three rabbits go
to Peter's house.

"We can have lunch now,"
says Peter's mother.

"We can eat radishes for
lunch!" says Cotton-tail.

"Radishes?" says Peter.

"I have got your three radishes!" says Cotton-tail.

"Cotton-tail!" says Peter. "YOU are the radish robber!"

Activities

The key below describes the skills practiced in each activity.

 Spelling and writing

 Reading

 Speaking

 Critical thinking

 Preparation for the Cambridge Young Learners Exams

1 Choose the correct answers.

1  This is
(**a** Peter Rabbit.)
b Mr. Tod.

2 This is
a Squirrel Nutkin.
b Benjamin.

3  This is
a Cotton-tail.
b Lily.

4 This is
a Mr. Tod.
b Mr. McGregor.

5 These are
a radishes.
b rabbits.

2 **Look and read. Write _yes_ or _no_.**

"Run!" says Peter.

The two rabbits run from Mr. McGregor.

They have got three radishes.

8

9

1 "Run!" says Mr. McGregor. ......no......

2 "Run!" says Benjamin. ....

3 Peter and Benjamin run from Mr. McGregor. ....

4 Mr. McGregor runs from the two rabbits. ....

5 Peter and Benjamin have got two radishes. ....

3 Look and read. Put a ✓ or a ✗ in the boxes.

1 Mr. McGregor has got a garden. ✓

2 There are radishes in the garden. ☐

3 Peter Rabbit does not want radishes. ☐

4 Benjamin wants radishes. ☐

5 Lily likes radishes. ☐

4 Circle the correct pictures.

1 Who goes with Peter to Mr. McGregor's garden?

 a   b

2 How many radishes do they take from his garden?

a    b

3 Who would like one of Peter and Benjamin's radishes?

a    b

4 Who says, "You cannot eat them here!"?

a    b

5 Write *Who* or *What*. 📖 ✏️

1 _____Who_____ goes to Mr. McGregor's garden with Peter?

2 _____ do Peter and Benjamin want?

3 _____ do Peter and Benjamin run from?

4 _____ have Peter and Benjamin got?

5 _____ is the radish robber?

6 Who says this?

Benjamin Cotton-tail Peter Lily

1 "Would you like a radish, Lily?"

Peter

2 "We have no radishes now."

3 "A robber has got mine!"

4 "Where is my radish?"

5 "We can eat radishes for lunch!"

7 Look and read. Complete the sentences. Write a—d. 📖

1 Peter and Benjamin go ......b......

2 Peter's mother is ....

3 Cotton-tail is ....

4 "Go and play," says ....

a Peter's mother.

b to Peter's house.

c in the kitchen.

d with Benjamin and Peter.

8 **Read the text. Write words to complete the sentences.** 📖 ✏️

> They go to Squirrel Nutkin's tree.
>
> "Let's eat the radishes here," says Peter.
>
> "No, you cannot eat them here!" says Squirrel Nutkin.

---

tree   Nutkin   radishes   here   eat

The three rabbits go to Squirrel

Nutkin's ¹ ___tree___ .

"Let's eat the ² _____

here," says Peter.

"No, you cannot ³ _____

them ⁴ _____ !" says

Squirrel ⁵ _____ .

9 Look at the picture. Put a ✓ or a ✗ in the boxes.

They go to Squirrel Nutkin's tree.

"Let's eat the radishes here," says Peter.

"No, you cannot eat them here!" says Squirrel Nutkin.

1 Lily and Benjamin are in Squirrel Nutkin's tree. ✓

2 Cotton-tail is in Squirrel Nutkin's tree.

3 Peter wants to eat the radishes in the tree.

4 Lily sees two radishes.

10 Circle the best answers. 📖 ❓

1 Does Lily want to eat a radish?

    a Yes, she does.

    b No, she does not.

2 What does a robber do?

    a A robber takes something from
       a person.

    b A robber gives something
       to a person.

3 Does Peter know the radish robber?

    a Yes, he does.

    b No, he does not.

4 What does the radish robber
   do with the radishes?

    a She takes them to her
       mother for lunch.

    b She eats them.

11 Find the words.

tree
eat
go
radishes

12 **Ask and answer questions about the picture with a friend.** 🗨 ⭐

"On, no! It is Mr. Tod!" says Peter.

"Run!" says Lily.

1 *How many rabbits does Mr. Tod see?*

Mr. Tod sees three rabbits.

2 How many radishes has Peter got?

3 How many radishes has Benjamin got?

4 What does Lily say?

13 **Look and read. Choose the correct words, and write them on the lines.** 📖 ✏️ ⭐

The three rabbits run from Mr. Tod.

"We have no radishes now," says Benjamin.

"A robber has got our radishes," says Lily.

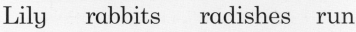

Lily   rabbits   radishes   run

1 The three ___rabbits___ run from Mr. Tod.

2 "We have no _____ now," says Benjamin.

3 "A robber has got our radishes," says _____.

4 The three rabbits _____ to Peter's house.

14 **Look, match, and write the words.**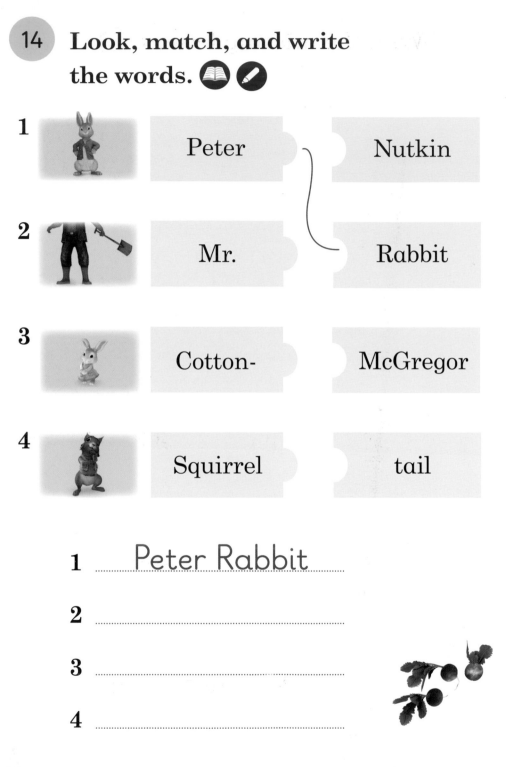

1   Peter — Rabbit

2   Mr. — Nutkin / Rabbit

3   Cotton- — McGregor

4   Squirrel — tail

1 Peter Rabbit

2

3

4

15 Write the missing letters. ✏️

(bb) (rr) (tt)

1 ra b b its

2 ro_____e r

3 Squi_____el Nutkin

4 Co_____on-tail

5 Peter Ra_____it

Order the story. Write 1—5.

.... The two rabbits run from Mr. McGregor with three radishes.

.... Lily wants her radish.

.... Cotton-tail is the radish robber!

_____1_____ Peter and Benjamin go to Mr. McGregor's garden.

.... Peter has got two radishes.

17 **Read the text and circle the correct answers.** 📖 ✿

The three rabbits go to Peter's house.

"We can have lunch now," says Peter's mother.

"We can eat radishes for lunch!" says Cotton-tail.

24   25

1 The three rabbits go to

a Peter's house.

b Mr. McGregor's garden.

2 "We can have lunch now," says

a Peter.

b Peter's mother.

3 They have . . . for lunch.

a radishes

b bread

18 Do the crossword. 📖 ✏️

Down

1 Peter is a . . .

2 The . . . robber

4 The rabbits . . .
from Mr. Tod.

Across

2 Cotton-tail is
the radish . . .

5 Peter's mother has
got three radishes
for their . . .

19 **Talk to a friend about rabbits.**
Answer the questions. 💬 ❓

1

Do you like rabbits?

Yes, I do.

2 Do rabbits like gardens?

3 What do rabbits eat?

4 Do people like rabbits in their gardens? Why? / Why not?

Level 1

Level 1
Anansi Helps a Friend
978-0-241-25409-7 ☐

Level 1
Cinderella
978-0-241-25407-3 ☐

Level 1
The Enormous Turnip
978-0-241-25408-0 ☐

Level 1
On the Farm
978-0-241-25413-4 ☐

Level 1
Cars
978-0-241-28354-7 ☐

Level 1
Jon's Football Team
978-0-241-25411-0 ☐

Level 1
The Magic Porridge Pot
978-0-241-25406-6 ☐

Level 1
In the Garden
978-0-241-26220-7 ☐

Level 1
Fun with Old Things
978-0-241-26219-1 ☐

Level 1
Fairy Friends
978-0-241-28351-6 ☐

Level 1
Peter Rabbit Goes to the Island
978-0-241-25415-8 ☐

Level 1
Topsy and Tim Go to the Zoo
978-0-241-25414-1 ☐

Level 1
Topsy and Tim Go to the Farm
978-0-241-28355-4 ☐

Level 1
The Fair
978-0-241-28357-8 ☐

Level 1
Daddy Pig's Old Chair
978-0-241-28356-1 ☐

Level 1
Rex the Big Dinosaur
978-0-241-29741-4 ☐

Level 1
Peter Rabbit and the Radish Robber
978-0-241-29742-1 ☐

Level 1
Topsy and Tim Go to London
978-0-241-29743-8 ☐

Level 1
On a Boat
978-0-241-29744-5 ☐

Level 1
Baby Animals
978-0-241-29745-2 ☐

Now you're ready for Level 2!